For Esme and Henry and for Jess, my super supportive mum —SC
For Max and Matthew —GM

Text copyright © 2020 by Stephanie Clarkson

Illustrations copyright © 2020 by Gwen Millward

Nosy Crow and its logos are trademarks of Nosy Crow Ltd. Used under license.

First US edition 2021

First published by Nosy Crow Ltd. (UK) 2020

Library of Congress Catalog Card Number pending

ISBN 978-1-5362-1726-1

21 22 23 24 25 26 APS 10 9 8 7 6 5 4 3 2 1

Printed in Humen, Dongguan, China

This book was typeset in Scotch Deck.

The illustrations were created digitally.

Nosy Crow

an imprint of

Candlewick Press

99 Dover Street

Somerville, Massachusetts 02144

www.nosycrow.com

www.candlewick.com

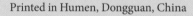

Super Milly and the Super School Day

STEPHANIE CLARKSON

ILLUSTRATED BY GWEN MILLWARD

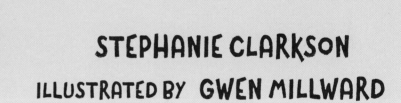

nosy crow

An imprint of Candlewick Press

I am **SUPER MILLY!**

Today is Superhero Day at school.

I have used all the tinfoil,
a tea towel with only one hole—
which doesn't even show—
a pair of my brother Joe's underwear,
and a sticker with an *M*.

But . . .

I don't have
X-ray vision.

I can't climb
buildings.

And superheroes are supposed to
beat the villains . . .

but I can't even stop Joe from taking
the last piece of toast.

I don't have any special powers.

When I get to school, there is already an emergency.

William's mom forgot that it is Superhero Day. I see him wearing his normal clothes and crying in the book corner.

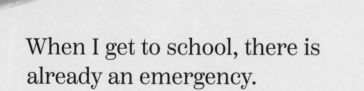

A real superhero would
spin around William
super fast . . .

until his outfit changed.

But Miss Kent says, "Bottoms
on seats, please."

So I think hard and . . .

I peel off my special sticker.

"You can be Wonder William," I say.
"But it's an *M*," he says.
I stick it on him upside down.
"Now it's a *W*!"

BAM!

Wonder William says
I am super kind.

Next, we have to write about
"A Day in the Life of a Superhero."

Fantastic Flora does not like writing.

Her *d*'s keep looking like *b*'s.

A real superhero would use
mega mind power . . .

to make Flora's pencil
write all by itself!

But the pencil stays still.

I think really hard and . . .

"Hey, Flora!" I say. "What has a cape and goes round and round?

A superhero in a washing machine."

KABOOM!

Fantastic Flora says I am super funny and writes down the joke all by herself.

In the afternoon, we do art.

Amazing Archie wants to paint a super villain,
but Spider Sid is hogging the green paint.

A real superhero would
grab the green . . .

and fly at super speed
between Archie and Sid
so they can share.

But my flying cape
is trapped under
my apron!

I think really,
really hard and . . .

"We can mix blue and yellow together to make green!" I say.

ZAP!

Amazing Archie is amazed and says I am super clever!

He loves green so much he paints
everything—including William!

It is almost time to go home.

Incredible Iqbal has brought in a minibeast for show-and-tell. Spider Sid says it's not even a tarantula. Iqbal's voice goes all quiet . . .

and then the spider escapes!

There is a lot of screaming . . .

until Fantastic Flora
catches it.

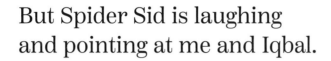

But Spider Sid is laughing
and pointing at me and Iqbal.

A real superhero would make a
force field around us so no one
can hurt our feelings.

But it's hard to do force fields when you are turning as red as a tomato.

I do some supersonic thinking and . . .

have a brilliant idea!
I hold hands with Iqbal, and our
superness gets stronger . . .

Then, in my loudest voice, I tell the class
that spiders have blue blood and can spin
silk. Iqbal's voice comes back, and he spells
out the name for the fear of spiders:

"A-R-A C-H-N-O-P-H-O-B-I-A."

WHIZZ!

Incredible Iqbal says
I am super brave.

WHAM!

Everyone claps and says
I am a super good friend.

Even Spider Sid
gives a loud cheer.

I am **SUPER MILLY!**

Maybe I *do* have special powers after all . . .

BAM!

I am kind.

KABOOM!

I am funny.

ZAP!

I am clever.

WHIZZ!
I am brave.

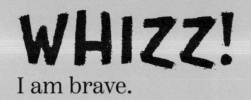

WHAM!
I am a good friend.

These are my
superpowers!

KERPOW!
I bet you have superpowers, too.